. . . and they love riding on them.

Grandpa used to be a train driver, and Dexter's
going to drive trains, too, when he's big enough.
He's already really good at staying awake during
long journeys, and spotting things out of the
window as they whizz past.
Today he's seen:

Flying Buffalo

three cows,

six sheep,

A day out with the Animal Railway

Sharon Rentta

CHOO - CHOO

ALISON GREEN BOOKS

Dexter loves trains.
So does his grandpa.

They like big trains,
small trains, fast trains,
slow trains, and all sorts
of trains in between.
They like watching them . . .

some flying pigs,

a horse in a
new coat,

two train-spotting
goats

and an elephant
in a paddling pool.

You have to buy a ticket before you get on a train. It's best to allow plenty of time. Grandpa and Dexter want to catch the Zebra Express, but it leaves in five minutes.

If only all those hamsters
would hurry up!

Dexter keeps all his tickets as souvenirs.

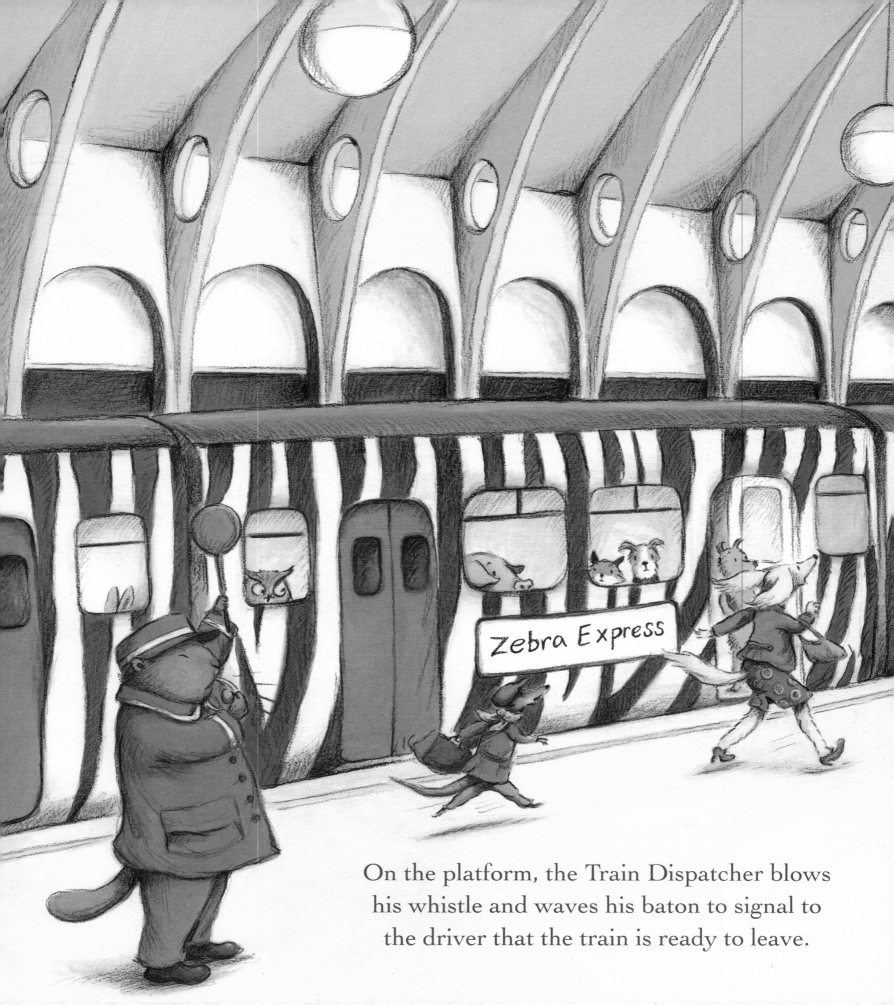

On the platform, the Train Dispatcher blows his whistle and waves his baton to signal to the driver that the train is ready to leave.

Grandpa and Dexter have to sprint or they'll miss it.
"That's the most exercise I've had in a while," puffs Grandpa.

There are so many passengers on the train that
Grandpa and Dexter have to stand. It's all a bit of a squash.

Dexter finds it's less crowded if you climb to the top of the handrail.

On a train, it's important not to:
swing from the luggage racks,

Blah!

Blah!

Blah!

put your feet on the seats,

or shout very loudly
into your mobile phone.

This crocodile is being
very selfish. He's hogged
three seats to himself,
but no one feels like
arguing with him.

Sometimes trains are delayed.
This train has broken down. The engineers are trying to work
out what's wrong, but so far they're all just scratching their heads.

This train is delayed because some cows
are having their dinner in the middle of the track.
They say they're very sorry to hold everyone up, but they
can't budge until they've finished chewing.

On cold days, the points can freeze up, which means that trains can't move from one track to another. All the trains come to a standstill until the problem's fixed.

Track Maintenance usually chip at the ice with chisels or melt it with a blow torch. Chief Engineer Bison reckons the best way to help out is by throwing snowballs.

Frozen points are a right headache for Doris in the Signal Box. She's got trains stuck all over the place, and everyone's getting grumpy.

When the trains finally start moving again, they're really packed. Grandpa and Dexter manage to squish inside, but other passengers aren't so lucky.

The Guard says the train isn't going anywhere until everyone clinging on the outside gets off. They'll all have to wait for the next train, which isn't for another hour.

It's much more fun travelling on a steam train.
This is the Huffer-Puffer Mountain Express.
The train lets out a massive blast of steam,
the whistle sounds: Whooo-whooo!
And off they go!

It's the
Fireman's job
to shovel coal
into the
fire box.
The fire heats
the water
which makes
the steam.
It's really hot,
dirty work.

Trains definitely go faster
if you make engine noises:
CHUFF
chuff
chuff
chuff
CHUFF!

Sleeper trains are exciting, too.

The train travels through the night while you're asleep. Dexter and Grandpa have their very own cabin with two bunks.

The bunks are reasonably bouncy
– but the ceiling's a bit low.

Ouch!

A story and a cuddle
with Grandpa sorts
out the problem.

ZZZZ

Then it's time to sleep.

Turns out they didn't need
both bunks after all.

One day, Dexter and Grandpa are sitting on a train waiting to go to the seaside.

They wait.

Typical, eh?!

And they wait.
But the train doesn't move.

Everyone's getting a bit fidgety,
so Dexter starts a cats' chorus.
Some other cats soon join in.

Mee-e-ow!!

That should keep everyone entertained.

This is why the train is delayed:

Marvin the Driver was hopping into his cab . . .

Crack!

. . . when he accidentally sat on his glasses! Oh, no! He can't drive the train without glasses!

Terry the Train Guard says Marvin's a silly sausage. If they can't find another driver, they'll have to cancel the train. Poor Marvin is very embarrassed.

Terry makes an announcement to the passengers:

THIS TRAIN IS DELAYED, AWAITING A NEW DRIVER. WE APOLOGISE FOR ANY INCONVENIENCE.

what!?

Everyone is very cross – except for Dexter.
"*You're* a driver, Grandpa!" he says.
"*You* can drive the train!"

Grandpa isn't so sure, but Dexter runs right up to Terry, and tells him that his grandpa is the best train driver in the world and he's going to drive the train right now.

Marvin is very relieved. Terry seems quite pleased, too.

Grandpa and Dexter each put on a hat,
to make them look like proper train drivers.
Then they climb into the cab and Grandpa
tells Dexter what all those knobs and dials do.
Dexter soon reckons he's got the hang of it.

In no time at all, they're speeding along the track,
all the way to . . .

. . . the seaside!

"Great driving, Dexter!" says Grandpa.
"I think we both deserve an ice cream!"

For the Wilkinson family,
who enjoy spotting a train or two.

First published in the UK in 2017 by Alison Green Books
An imprint of Scholastic Children's Books
Euston House, 24 Eversholt Street, London NW1 1DB
A division of Scholastic Ltd
www.scholastic.co.uk
London – New York – Toronto – Sydney – Auckland
Mexico City – New Delhi – Hong Kong

Copyright © 2017 Sharon Rentta

HB ISBN: 978 1 407171 79 1
PB ISBN: 978 1 407171 80 7